Class Trip

SCHOLASTIC INC.

ISBN 978-0-545-52402-5

Published by arrangement with Entertainment One and Ladybird Books, A Penguin Company.

This book is based on the TV series *Peppa Pig*.

Peppa Pig is created by Neville Astley and Mark Baker.

Peppa Pig © Astley Baker Davies Ltd/Entertainment One UK Ltd 2003.

12 11 10 9 8 7 6 5 4 3 2 1   13 14 15 16 17 18/0

Printed in the U.S.A.   40

This edition first Scholastic printing, August 2013

www.peppapig.com

Peppa and her friends are
going on a class trip.

Woof!

"Let's check that you are all here,"
says Madame Gazelle.
"Here!" cries Peppa.

Baaa! Grunt! Snort!

"Today," says Madame Gazelle, "we are going on a trip to the mountains!"

"Hooray!"
cheer all the children.

Peppa and Suzy are already a little hungry.
"Can we eat our lunches now, please?"
they ask Madame Gazelle.

"Why don't you eat your apples and save the rest for our picnic?" the teacher replies. Crunch! Crunch!

The bus has arrived at the foot of
the mountain. The road is very steep!
"Come on, bus! You can make it!"
everyone cheers.

Peppa and her friends have finally made it
to the top of the mountain.
"Look at the view!" gasps Madame Gazelle.
All the children look out over the valley.

"Wow!" exclaims Peppa loudly.
"Wow! Wow! Wow!" Peppa hears
in the distance.
"What was that?" she asks.
"It's your echo, Peppa!"
replies Madame Gazelle.

Wow!

Wow!

Wow!

The kids all take turns making
noises to hear their echoes.
Grunt! Woof! Baaa! Snort!

Now it's time for a picnic lunch.
Peppa loves picnics. Everyone loves
picnics! *Munch! Slurp! Crunch!*
Yum! Yum!

"Where are the ducks?" asks Peppa, taking a bite of her sandwich. "They always turn up when we have picnics."

Quack! Quack! Quack! Here come the ducks.
"Hello! Would you like some bread?" Peppa asks them.

The ducks are very lucky today. The kids brought plenty of extra bread to feed them!

Everyone hops back on the bus. It's time to go home.

"Let's all sing a song!" suggests
Madame Gazelle. La, la, la.

Everyone has had a great day!